To my husband Steven, Harley and Portia for bringing
love, laughter and roots into my life.

To the Junior Master Gardener® Program and its innovative evidence-based
Learn, Grow, Eat & GO! curriculum for enriching the health,
well-being and academic success of children worldwide.
Visit jmgkids.us to learn more.

And to all tiny seeds everywhere–just relax, smile and be loved
while enjoying the ride home! – **SB**

To Skutch–the hardest worker I know. – **KM**

a place
to grow

has a place on the Web!
www.placetogrow.com

Bloom & Grow Books

A Division of Bloom & Grow, Inc.
17412 Ventura Blvd. #373
Los Angeles, CA 91316

A Place to Grow and Bloom & Grow are exclusive trademarks of
Bloom & Grow, Inc.

Copyright © 2002 by Stephanie Bloom

All rights reserved. No part of this publication may be reproduced
or transmitted in any form or by any means, electronic or
mechanical, including photocopying, recording, or by any
information storage and retrieval system, without the prior
written permission of the Publisher, unless otherwise expressly
permitted by federal copyright law.

Designed by Kiku Obata & Company
Edited by Nancy Parent
Printed and bound by CG Book Printers
Special thanks to Eleanor and Robert Bloom

Library of Congress Control Number:
2002090002

ISBN-13: 978-1-93196-907-9

Printed and bound in the United States of America
20 19 18 17 16   6 5 4 3 2

Enjoy your journey at www.bloomandgrow.com!

a place to grow

Written by Stephanie Bloom

Illustrated by Kelly Murphy

Bloom & Grow Books

The tiny seed floated down from the sky and

Could this be my place to grow?

The tiny seed wondered.

landed on the earth without a sound.

I hope so.
For as long as I can remember,
I have been searching for a home.

Where had it
landed this time?

The ground was shady and cool. It
buckled and cracked, like something
was pushing from deep inside.

"Whoa!"

exclaimed the tiny seed.
It had landed at the foot
of an enormous tree.

"This looks like the perfect place
for me to put down roots."

"Looks can be deceiving,"
replied the tree in a voice so deep it made
the ground hum. "This forest is no place for
a little seed to grow. My roots are so tangled
and thirsty, you would never get enough
soil or water. And my branches are so
broad, they would steal all your sunlight.
You could never grow here."

"I will never grow anywhere," sighed the seed.

"Yes, you will," chuckled the big tree, "because that's what seeds do—we
grow. It happens to all of us. One day you will find the place that's right
for you. It will have everything you need to take root. Until then, enjoy
your journey my little friend."

"Oh, Wind!"
called the tiny seed.
"Please come and get me.
This is not my place to grow."

So the Wind blew in and

carried the tiny seed far, far away.

The tiny seed floated down from the sky and landed or

Could this be my place to grow?

The tiny seed wondered.

Where had it landed this time? A buzzing bee danced from flower to flower, darting back in surprise at seeing butterflies.

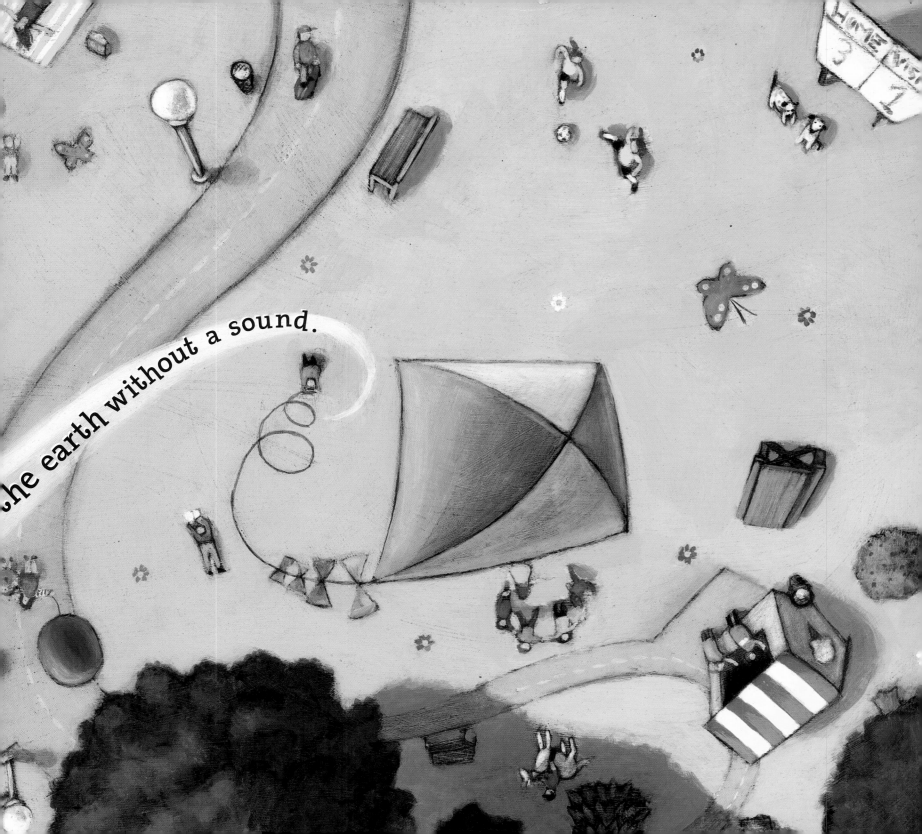

...he earth without a sound.

So the Wind blew in and

OOᵒf!

The tiny seed was moving! A giant ant had snatched it up and was racing toward a big pile of sand.

"Stop! Put me down!" yelled the seed.

"Oh my! Oh my!" wheezed the ant. "I thought you were a pebble. I was going to use you on top of my anthill. You would make a dandy front door."

"I'm no pebble," snapped the seed. "I'm a seed waiting to grow. Can't you see that?"

"This park is a busy, busy place and I am a busy, busy ant. I don't have time to notice *everything*." And with that, the ant hurried back to its home.

I wish I could build a home like the ant, thought the tiny seed. *But a seed needs roots, not sand and pebbles.*

"Oh, Wind!" called the tiny seed. "This is not my place to grow. Please come and get me."

carried the tiny seed far, far away.

The tiny seed floated down from

...he sky and landed on the earth without a sound.

Could this be my place to grow?

The tiny seed wondered.

Where had it
landed this time?
Silky tufts of clover blanketed
the fresh green pasture.

CHOMP!
CHOMP!
CHOMP!

The tiny seed looked up
and gasped. A cow's huge,
wet tongue was heading
straight toward it!

"Watch where you're eating!"
hollered the seed. "You
almost made me your lunch!"

CHOMP!   CHOMP!
          CHOMP!

"Hey, cow! Did you hear me?"
But the hungry cow just kept on chewing.

CHOMP! CHOMP! CHOMP!
                GULP!   BUUUURRRPPP!

The cow licked its lips
and leaned down to take another bite...

Just as the tiny seed was about to be eaten,   the Wind blew in and carried it far, far away.

Could this be my place to grow?

The tiny seed wondered.

Where had it landed this time?
A weathered wooden fence guarded rows and rows of ripe vegetables.

The tiny seed floated down from the sky

and landed on the earth without a sound.

"**Scram!**" barked a red tomato.

"Every spot's taken!" screeched a yellow pepper.

"What about over there?" asked the tiny seed, pointing to an empty patch of soil. "I promise I will grow so quietly, you'll never know I'm here."

"**Well,**" boomed a plump, purple eggplant, "that row is for rutabagas. **Are you a rutabaga?**"

"Hmmm...I don't know," replied the seed. "I don't even know if I'm a vegetable."

"We knew what kind of seeds we were right from the start," squeaked a green zucchini. "A gardener brought us home from the greenhouse in packets with our names on them."

"Then I'm definitely not a vegetable," said the seed sadly. "I don't come from a packet, I float down from the sky. And I'm not planted by a gardener, I have to plant myself."

"In that case," boomed the eggplant, "you can't grow in our garden. We're sorry, but you just don't belong here."

"This is not my place to grow," said the seed very softly.

And without having to be asked,

the Wind blew in and carried the tiny seed far, far away.

The tiny seed cried as the Wind

gently cradled it in its swirling current.

"You must never lose hope," whispered the Wind.

"But I have searched and searched,"
the tiny seed sobbed, "and there is no place
for me to grow. I will never find a home."

"For as long as time," whispered the Wind, "I have carried
all kinds of seeds across the earth. And one by one,
each seed found its own special place to grow."

"But I'm not like other seeds.
I'm a floater, not a grower."

"You are a grower," whispered the Wind,
"because that's what seeds do—they grow."

"You sound just like the old tree,"
said the seed.

"The old tree was once a tiny seed and rode with me
just like you," whispered the Wind.
"Now, it's time for you to float down
to the ground and look again."

"No, Wind!
I want to stay here with you!
Please don't let me go!" cried the tiny seed.

"Don't be afraid. You will find your place to grow and blossom.
And I will be there. I will always be there," whispered the Wind,
gently releasing the tiny seed from its airy embrace.

The tiny seed floated down from

Could this *be my place to grow?*

The tiny seed wondered.

Where had it
landed this time?
Giant hills rolled up to the clouds, filling
the valley below with a peaceful calm.

Exhausted from all its adventures,
the tiny seed yawned and fell sound asleep.

the sky and landed on the earth without a sound.

Choo Chooo Choooo!

A puffing steam engine roared by
and spun the tiny seed high up into the air!

"One minute I was dreaming of growing,
and now I can't tell up from down!" shouted the seed.
"This is definitely NOT my place to grow!
Wind, *please* come and get me!"

So the Wind blew in

and carried the tiny seed far, far away.

I'm sure this is not my place to grow, thought the tiny seed. It never is.

Where had it landed this time?

Blades of tall, shiny grass
swayed as if waving hello,
while a bubbly band of crickets
chirped a welcome song.

*Soon I will discover the reason why
this place can't be my home. Then I will be
soaring through the sky again.*

The tiny seed floated down from

the sky and landed on the earth without a sound.

So the tiny seed waited...

And waited.

And waited.

And waited.

While the tiny seed waited
in the grassy meadow,
the sun streamed
through the clouds.

"Aah, the sunlight is
so warm here,"
sighed the seed, bathing
in the golden glow.

Later, a light rain showered down.
"Mmm, the water is so sweet here,"
said the seed as it drank and
drank and drank.

Soon the rain stopped.
"Ooh, the soil is so soft here,"
sang the seed, snuggling
into the moist earth.

Then the tiny seed
felt the Wind blow into the meadow.
And although it loved the Wind,
the seed was filled with
a deep sadness at having to
leave this place and float again.

The Wind blew. And blew. And blew.

But a strange thing happened.
The seed *didn't* float up into the sky
and the Wind *didn't* carry it far, far away.
The tiny seed couldn't move. It was held firmly
in place by a root that was as strong as it was small.

The tiny seed was growing at last!

"Oh, Wind," shouted the seed with joy.
"I have finally found my place to grow!
I belong HERE in this grassy meadow!"

"You are home," the Wind whispered back.
"Enjoy your new journey."

And there in the grassy meadow,
the tiny seed grew...

And grew.

And grew.

And grew.

the beginning...